D1650026

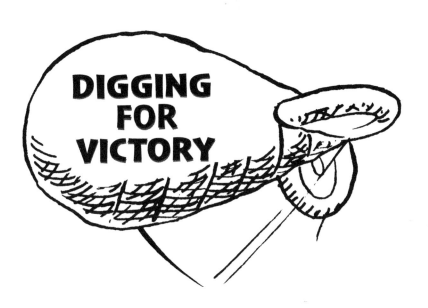

DIGGING FOR VICTORY

by Jack Wood
Ilustrations by Tim Sell

W
FRANKLIN WATTS
LONDON•SYDNEY

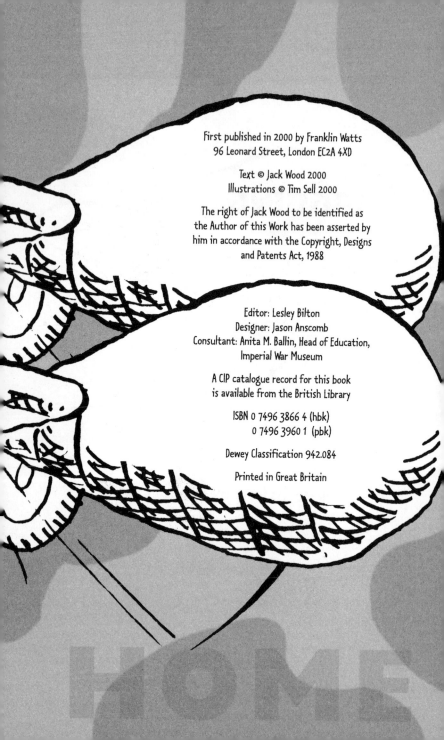

First published in 2000 by Franklin Watts
96 Leonard Street, London EC2A 4XD

Text © Jack Wood 2000
Illustrations © Tim Sell 2000

Editor: Lesley Bilton
Designer: Jason Anscomb
Consultant: Anita M. Ballin, Head of Education,
Imperial War Museum

A CIP catalogue record for this book
is available from the British Library

ISBN 0 7496 3866 4 (hbk)
0 7496 3960 1 (pbk)

Dewey Classification 942.084

Printed in Great Britain

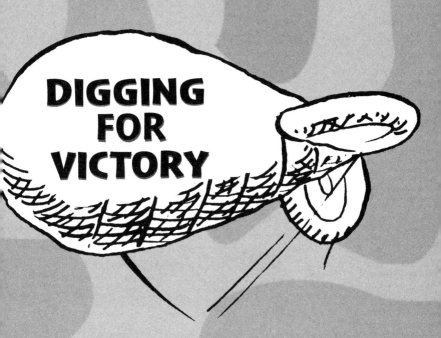

DIGGING FOR VICTORY

by Jack Wood
Ilustrations by Tim Sell

TALES OF THE SECOND WORLD WAR

Chapter 1

A Grave Lesson

"Do you know why they give us lessons in this churchyard?" asked Eddie.

"No." Roy looked up from his exercise book.

"It'll save money. When a bomb drops on us, they won't have to pay for our funeral."

It made sense, thought Roy, leaning back against a stone angel. Since their school had been bombed, they'd had lessons in some funny places, but Saint Cuthbert's churchyard was the funniest.

Roy closed his book and studied the sky. Above him, the barrage balloons drifted, like silver whales on strings. Lenny, his older brother, said they were supposed to stop low-flying enemy planes. But balloons wouldn't stop him, Roy decided, when he was old enough to join the air force. He could imagine exactly how he'd fly round them . . .

Squadron Leader Roy "Hawkeye" Pitt, weaved his plane between the enemy barrage balloons with ease. KERUMP! – his bombs landed dead on target. Skilfully dodging the fire from the anti-aircraft guns, he looked down on the blazing German factory with satisfaction. "Bullseye!" he yelled over the intercom. "Let's head for home, chaps..."

"Bet you haven't got anything to eat," said Eddie, rummaging in his bag. "I've got a sandwich."

"*I've* got an orange."

"Don't believe you."

Roy gave a smug smile, dug in his pocket, and brought out an orange. Carelessly, he tossed it in the air.

Eddie's eyes widened. "Where did you get *that*?"

"Stan Figg, the greengrocer, is soppy about my sister Joanie. Last night he gave her three oranges and a banana."

"Jammy thing," said Eddie. He stuffed a slab of bread into his mouth, chewed once, pulled a face, then spat it out with a cough. "Urgh, Spam!"

With a shudder, he flung away the remains

of his sandwich. It landed with a plop on the grave of Solomon Pepper.

Roy was shocked. "That's waste! You could have given it to me. I like Spam."

"Take it," said Eddie, grabbing Roy's orange. "I'll do a swop."

"Don't you dare!" Roy threw himself at Eddie and knocked him to the ground. The orange flew out of his hand, rolled across the grass, and disappeared under a door in the church wall.

Picking himself up, Eddie raced after it,

and twisted the rusty handle of the door.

"Edgar Leek, what are you doing in Saint Cuthbert's vestry?"

Eddie whirled round, and his eyes met the glare of their teacher, Miss Lemon. She was standing behind a tombstone, and looked like a skeleton that had risen from the grave.

"Er . . . I was looking at the old church, miss," stammered Eddie. He stared hard at the open door. "History, miss."

It was a good try, but it didn't work.

"This is supposed to be a *maths* lesson." The teacher hugged the pile of books she was carrying closer to her bony chest.

Miss Lemon was about a hundred years old – all the younger teachers had left to do something useful in the war. They should have sent her off to fight too, thought Roy. The Germans would have surrendered straight away.

"Day dreaming again, Roy Pitt?" Her voice was sour. "I suppose it's too much to expect any work from a member of your family."

Miss Lemon had taught his Dad and Lenny, and she didn't think much of the Pitts.

"Finished, miss," said Roy, handing her his book.

Her face fell. As she added it to the pile, her beady eyes darted around, searching for something to complain about. She didn't have far to look. With a trembling finger, she pointed at Eddie's chewed sandwich. "To whom does this food belong?"

"Please, miss, it's mine. I don't want it. I don't like Spam."

Miss Lemon exploded like a time bomb. "Wicked waste! How dare you spurn Supply

Pressed American Meat? You are helping
Hitler to win the war. Come with me!"

After Eddie had been frog-marched away,
Roy turned back to the grave of Solomon
Pepper and eyed the remains of the Spam
sandwich hungrily. Several flies were buzzing
round the smooth slices of pink tinned meat
that stuck out of the bread. With a regretful
sigh, Roy decided to leave the sandwich where
it was.

His stomach rumbling, he headed for
home. What could Ma have found for dinner
tonight? Ever since food rationing had begun,

they'd had less meat, but as the war dragged on, lots of other things had become scarce as well.*

He hoped it wasn't vegetable pie – they'd had that for the last three days. *Anything* would be better than vegetable pie. Perhaps Gran's chickens had laid some eggs, and Ma had been lucky in the butcher's queue. Maybe there'd even be sausages!

* *Read more about food rationing on page 60*

Chapter 2
A Fruitful Discovery

Afternoon was darkening into early evening as Roy rounded the corner into Balaclava Terrace. Mrs Moon, the Pitts' next-door neighbour, was standing on the pavement, staring anxiously at her house.

"HUBERT," she screamed.

The bedroom curtain was pulled back, revealing the fat face of her son. He opened

the window and leaned out. "WHAT'S THE MATTER NOW?"

"THERE'S LIGHT SHOWING AT THE TOP! PULL THE CURTAINS CLOSER TOGETHER!" She took a few steps backwards and bumped into Roy.

"Oh, it's you. Tell your Dad and that layabout Lenny to get on with the blackout. You Pitts are a disgrace! You'll get the whole street blown up! You'll –"

Roy ducked passed her and ran into his house. Once she started complaining, Mrs Moon (known to the whole street, for obvious reasons, as Mrs Moan) could carry on for hours.

But she had a point. Light streamed from the windows of Number 46. Shaking his head, Roy shut the door carefully behind him, and pulled tight the black concealing curtain.

"Home, Ma," he shouted, sniffing a hopeful sniff, as he hung his gas mask next to Dad's cap. But the only smell in the air was a green, damp, *familiar* smell. Surely it couldn't be vegetable pie *again*?

***

It was vegetable pie again. But no one complained. Quite the opposite! Gran, Dad, Ma, Lenny, Joanie and Heather joked and laughed – they behaved as if they were eating roast beef!

"You're all very cheerful," Roy said suspiciously, as Ma cleared away the remains.

"We've good reason," chuckled Dad, bending down under the table and dragging a

large crate into the middle of the room.

"What is it?" Roy asked.

"What does it look like?" Dad took a swig from his bottle of beer.

"A crate."

"Well, that's what it is. A crate of tins. Tinned fruit, if you must know, Mister Curiosity. Lenny just happened to find it," Dad winked at Lenny, "as he was walking home."

"Yeah," said Lenny. "Fell off the back of a lorry. Nearly did me a nasty injury."

Roy thought this over. "You ought to tell

the police. If they find out, you could be
arrested for dealing in the Black Market.
Suppose Mrs Moan sees it? She says you can
go to prison for two years, and –"

"We don't want to know what Mrs Moan
says," said Ma. She sighed and opened one of
the ration books in front of her. "Come over
here and help me add up these coupons."

"The boy's right about one thing," growled
Gran. "You never know when that busybody's
going to waltz into the house. Take the goods
to the allotment and hide them in the shed."

"The shed's full," said Joanie. She waved her hands in the air, trying to dry her nail polish. "It's full of those cans of black market petrol you got last week."

"Well, dig a hole and bury it." Gran stuck her nose back into her magazine.

Roy looked worried. "If anyone finds it –"

"Let me explain about the Black Market, Roy." Dad spat into the fire. "It's not really criminal like they make out in the posters. These tins are probably dented." He kicked the crate. "So we're doing everybody a favour by not letting them go to waste."

"Waste not, want not. Like the Government says," piped up Heather. She was cutting

old newspapers into small squares. Toilet paper had been scarce for ages.

"If it was left to the Government, we'd all starve," said Lenny, picking up one of the newspapers. "Listen to this." He put on a posh voice. "Mother – spoil your family tonight. Give them whale meat! Serve with a tasty dish of boiled nettles.* You'll have them clammering for more."

Dad gave a short laugh. "See what they expect us to eat, to hold body and soul together? Whales! Nettles!" He grabbed Lenny's paper and hurled it to the ground, knocking over his bottle of beer.

"We should be growing our own food," said Roy. "Digging for Victory. We haven't even dug the allotment over, let alone planted any seeds –"

"Sometimes I can't believe that you're a

Lots of strange foods were eaten during the war – see page 61

Pitt," barked Gran. "Do something useful for a change and help Lenny get rid of that crate."

Roy opened his mouth, but nobody heard what he said. All hell suddenly broke loose in the street outside.

Yells! Whistles! Bangs! More yells!

Then a very loud voice rose above the hubbub.

"EVERYBODY OUT OF THEIR HOUSES! EVACUATE YOUR HOMES NOW!"

GREEN VEGETABLES & SALADS
help you to resist infection clear the
skin and take the place of raw fruit

Chapter 3
To the Shelter

"Who's making that racket?" asked Dad.

Lenny flipped back a corner of the blackout curtain and peered out.

"This sticky tape on the windows may stop flying glass, but it's murder trying to see anything." He pulled the curtain wider open. "I think it's Boggy Marsh."

"Oh him," groaned Dad.

Mr Marsh, the local Air-Raid Precautions Warden, was not one of Dad's favourite people. "That man's more of a menace than Hitler. They've given him a whistle and a tin hat, and the power's gone to his head."

"PUT THAT LIGHT OUT, NUMBER 46! DON'T YOU KNOW THERE'S A WAR ON?" The voice from the street was so loud it made the window rattle.

Lenny dropped the curtain. "It looks serious. There's a policeman with him. I'll go and see what's up. Better cover that crate."

He slipped out of the door. Ma threw the beer-stained table cloth over the crate, and they all stared at it in silence.

Lenny wasn't long. "They've found an unexploded bomb. The whole street's being evacuated. We've got to leave our house and –"

"COME IMMEDIATELY. TAKE ONLY YOUR GAS MASK AND RATION BOOK. TURN OFF ALL ELECTRICITY, GAS AND WATER."

The Pitts straggled out into the road. It was chaos. Balaclava Terrace was full of confused people milling around. Boggy, puffed up with importance, was strutting up and down, bawling loudly. "COME ON. COME ON. LET'S BE HAVING YOU!"

He started dragging people into a line. "Two Moons, six Pratts, seven Pitts, five Hoggs, four –"

"Why are you counting us?"

"I've got to tell Heavy Rescue how many

ry it – better take Heather. Get the crate to
allotment. We'll bury it there. Joanie, deal
h that idiot of a warden."

"Sure thing, Dad," said Joanie. She
othed her dress with her hands, tossed her
, and glided over to Boggy. In the dim
of his covered torch, her hair gleamed

You're so brave, Warden Marsh," she
, taking him by the hand and swinging
und. "I bet you've saved hundreds of
's lives."

bodies to look for if the bomb goes off."

"We're all going to be killed!"

"Hold your noise, Queenie Moon. It'll take
more than a bomb to get rid of you."

Mrs Moan was dithering about on the
pavement outside her house. In one hand she
carried her budgie's cage, and with her other
hand she clutched Hubert.

"Where's Mrs Trotter? I –" Boggy broke

off, stopped counting the Trotters, and made a sudden dash down the road.

"There's no time for that, Grandad Grubb," he bawled, flinging himself on a wrinkled old man who was piling the contents of his house into a wheelbarrow.

Lenny pulled Dad and Roy aside. "What are we going to do about the fruit? That nosey warden could walk into the house tonight. It might be days before they let us come back home."

"It might be weeks. When a bomb dropped on my sister's road . . ."

Mrs Moan's voice faded away ? crocodile of people began to shuffl road.

"Where are we going?"
"To an Emergency Shelter."
"Where is it?"
"You'll know when you get
"Will there be anything to
"Shut up, Hubert Moon."
"I've forgotten my false t
"HURRY UP, YOU PITTS!"

Roy saw his chance to gain some glory. "Don't worry, Dad. I'll get the fruit. Just distract Boggy's attention while I slip back into the house."

Dad looked doubtful. "It'll need two of you to

ca
the
wit

sm
hea
glow
gold

cooe
him r
peopl

bodies to look for if the bomb goes off."

"We're all going to be killed!"

"Hold your noise, Queenie Moon. It'll take more than a bomb to get rid of you."

Mrs Moan was dithering about on the pavement outside her house. In one hand she carried her budgie's cage, and with her other hand she clutched Hubert.

"Where's Mrs Trotter? I –" Boggy broke

off, stopped counting the Trotters, and made a sudden dash down the road.

"There's no time for that, Grandad Grubb," he bawled, flinging himself on a wrinkled old man who was piling the contents of his house into a wheelbarrow.

Lenny pulled Dad and Roy aside. "What are we going to do about the fruit? That nosey warden could walk into the house tonight. It might be days before they let us come back home."

"It might be weeks. When a bomb dropped on my sister's road . . ."

Mrs Moan's voice faded away as the crocodile of people began to shuffle down the road.

"Where are we going?"

"To an Emergency Shelter."

"Where is it?"

"You'll know when you get there."

"Will there be anything to eat?"

"Shut up, Hubert Moon."

"I've forgotten my false teeth."

"HURRY UP, YOU PITTS!"

Roy saw his chance to gain some glory. "Don't worry, Dad. I'll get the fruit. Just distract Boggy's attention while I slip back into the house."

Dad looked doubtful. "It'll need two of you to

carry it – better take Heather. Get the crate to the allotment. We'll bury it there. Joanie, deal with that idiot of a warden."

"Sure thing, Dad," said Joanie. She smoothed her dress with her hands, tossed her head, and glided over to Boggy. In the dim glow of his covered torch, her hair gleamed gold.

"You're so brave, Warden Marsh," she cooed, taking him by the hand and swinging him round. "I bet you've saved hundreds of people's lives."

Boggy turned red and coughed. "Well, Miss Pitt, I've certainly –"

"Now!" said Dad.

Roy grabbed Heather by the hand and pulled her after him into the alley way which ran down one side of Number 46. Flattened against the wall of the passage, they waited until the procession of people had wound down the road.

When the final straggling figure had disappeared from sight, Roy made his move.

"Let Operation Fruit Rescue commence," he hissed to Heather. "I'm the officer-in-charge. You can be my second-in-command. Let's go! I'll follow you."

"Officers first," said Heather, with a sweet smile.

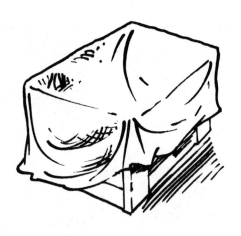

A clear plate
means
A clear conscience

Don't take more than you can eat

Chapter 4
A Rough Ride

Inside the house all was dark and silent.
Feeling their way carefully, Roy and Heather
edged into the front room. The outline of the
crate was visible in the glow shed by the dying
embers of the fire. Now for it!

Roy wrapped both his arms round the
wooden box and heaved. Nothing happened.

He tried again. Still nothing. It was no

good – he couldn't budge it. "Give me a hand," he ordered Heather.

For ten minutes the two of them tried to move the crate.

They pushed.

They pulled.

They pushed and pulled and heaved and tugged, but, although they could lift it, the crate was too heavy for them to carry any distance.

"What are we going to do?" Roy sank to his knees.

"Hang on. I've an idea," said Heather. She slipped out of the room, leaving Roy staring at the crate. How could he shift it? He should have listened to Ma. She said he'd never be strong if he didn't eat his greens.* And he'd need to be strong when he joined the army. Suppose he was stranded in the desert . . .

---

* *Eating lots of vegetables kept people healthy – see page 62*

"I can't go on," croaked Corporal Bean, as he slumped against the side of a broken-down tank. "Leave me here to die." The hot North African sun beat down on his exhausted body. Captain Roy "Bulldog" Pitt said nothing, but his mouth set in a firm line. Bending down, he lifted his comrade from the desert sand. "We'll make it together, old man," he muttered through gritted teeth . . .

"Wake up, Dolly Day-Dream." Heather's voice made him jump. "I thought we could use this." She was dragging her old pram into the room. "It was in the cupboard under the stairs. The wheels squeak, but it might do."

WAAAAAAAAAAAAAAAAAAAH!

The scream of the air-raid siren made them jump. Roy's heart sank.

Heather clutched his arm. "I'm scared," she said in a small voice. "I don't want to be killed by the Germans."

"We'll be killed by Dad if we don't rescue this fruit. Let's try lifting it together."

Fear gave them strength. With one giant heave, they hoisted the crate into the pram. Heather tucked a fluffy pink blanket around it, and stood back. "That'll do," she said. "Come on, I'll see if the coast's clear. Wait till I give the signal, then run for it."

She turned the handle of the front door and opened it a fraction. Above the sky was clear. The full moon shone brightly – a Bomber's Moon – making it easy for the German pilots to spot their targets. Far in the

distance, they could hear the drone of aeroplane engines. Anti-aircraft bullets exploded in the air, and swooping searchlights criss-crossed the sky. One of them lit up a figure in uniform standing at the end of the road.

"Policeman," Heather whispered over her shoulder. "He's put a barrier across the end of the Terrace. What shall we do?"

"How should I know?"

"You're supposed to be the officer. Any bright ideas, sir?"

Roy thought furiously. He gave the pram an experimental push. The wheels squeaked loudly. "We'll never get past him. Even if he doesn't see us, he'll hear us. Couldn't you distract him, like Joanie distracted Boggy? Pretend to be lost, or something?"

Heather stared at him thoughtfully. "OK, I'll try." She smoothed her coat, straightened her pixie hood, and nodded to Roy. "Operation Fruit Rescue – the second-in-command takes charge. If I don't come back, tell Dad I did my best."

Easing open the front door, she sneaked out and slid, like a small grey shadow, into the road. Roy, peering through the letterbox, saw her walk over to the policeman and tug his sleeve.

"Please help me, Mister. I'm frightened. I've lost my Ma." Sob, sob, sob.

It seemed to be working. The policeman bent down and said something to Heather. She carried on bawling her eyes out, and pointed towards the end of Balaclava Terrace. Taking her by the hand, the policeman began to walk slowly down the road.

Roy swallowed. It was up to him now – Operation Fruit Rescue had become a solo mission. He took a deep breath, launched the pram into the road, and pelted as fast as he could away from Heather and the policeman.

He didn't stop until he turned the corner into Alma Road. Then, as he paused for breath, the night went suddenly white.

Black. White. Black. White.

BANG! BANG! BANG! The crash of the anti-aircraft guns made his ears hurt. Then silence. Only the sound of a dog howling.

Chug-chug-chug-chug. A lone aircraft! It was German – he knew by the sound of its engine.

Roy began to panic. He'd never been caught above ground in an air raid before. He must find shelter. "Keep calm", he told himself as he scurried into Inkerman Road.

THUMP! Roy suddenly saw stars. He saw them because he was lying flat on his back, gazing up at the sky. He'd fallen into a bomb crater!

With a groan, he scrambled painfully to his hand and knees, and felt around for his glasses. They'd fallen into a muddy puddle. He fished them out, gave them a shake and jammed them on his nose, but they were so dirty he could hardly see the pram. It had banged into the wall, and one of its wheels looked bent. Roy was bending down to examine the damage when he heard a loud shout.

"HEY YOU THERE! WHAT DO YOU THINK YOU'RE DOING? DON'T YOU KNOW THERE'S A RAID ON?"

Oh no! There couldn't be two voices like that.

It was Warden Marsh!

CHAPTER 5
Blown Up!

Roy thought fast. If Boggy caught him, he'd be in trouble. If he caught him with the crate of fruit, he'd be in *deep* trouble. He must get rid of the pram. Quickly.

He took to his heels and veered off down a small side alley. At the end, he turned right, left and then left again. He bolted so fast that the rickety pram cornered on two wheels.

Sweating, he stopped for a moment in the shelter of an archway, and ran his fingers through his hair. It felt prickly. He wondered if it had turned white with shock. Odd shapes danced in front of his eyes. Perhaps that was another symptom of shock.

With a shaking hand, he took off his glasses, peered at them, and discovered the cause of his trouble. It wasn't shock – it was dirt! He spat on the lenses, wiped them on his shirt and hooked them back round his ears. That was better!

The archway he was leaning against was the entrance to Saint Cuthbert's – where his maths lesson had been earlier that day! It felt like a year ago.

He could hear Boggy's big feet pounding towards him. He was getting closer. Where could he hide the pram?

The vestry! Hadn't the door opened when Eddie pushed it? That would do!

Flying through the churchyard, he headed for the small door at the back of the church. The handle was stiff, and the door gave a massive screech when he pushed it – but it opened!

In whooshed the pram! Slam went the door!

And on round the church path whizzed Roy – straight into Boggy's waiting arms!

"Got you, you stupid child." He grabbed Roy by the collar and stared at him hard. "You're one of those Pitts, aren't you? What are you up to?" His eyes darted round the churchyard suspiciously. "Where's that pram you were pushing?"

Perhaps it wouldn't be too bad in prison, thought Roy.* The food couldn't be any worse than at home. Maybe Ma would be allowed to visit him.

* *Blackmarketeers could go to prison – see page 63*

An ear-splitting whistle drove all thoughts of prison from his head. He'd heard that sound many times before – but never so loud. It was a bomb!

The noise, half-moan and half-wail, ended in a shattering roar, and the blast wave sent Roy flying backwards. His head smacked with

a sickening thump against a tombstone. He wondered if it was Solomon Pepper's, but he couldn't see. And he couldn't breathe either!

He couldn't breathe because Boggy was lying on top of him. There was an awful lot of Boggy, and all of it was pressing down on his stomach.

CRASH! CRASH! CRASH! Billowing smoke filled the sky, and then the underside of the smoke-cloud turned vivid yellow.

"Crikey, that was a close one." Boggy scrambled to his feet. "Looks like my district. Off with you to a shelter, double-quick, my lad." He rushed off, his gas mask case bumping up and down against his bottom.

Gingerly Roy picked himself up and brushed the dirt off his trousers. He felt bone-weary. Lenny would have to pick up the crate tomorrow. He'd done his bit, he thought, as he limped out of the churchyard.

Chapter 6
A Fruitless Visit

It was light when Roy arrived at the allotment. The "all clear" had sounded some time ago, but it had been a dreadful night!

First he'd trudged all the way back to Balaclava Terrace, only to find that the street was still cordoned off.

Then he'd traipsed miles and miles, looking in all the big public shelters – but none of them contained any Pitts.

As a last resort, he headed for the allotment. And there they were!

Dad was digging a large hole. It was the first time he'd ever seen Dad digging, and he wasn't doing a bad job. Lenny and Heather were carting away the soil, while Ma and Joanie heaped the unearthed vegetables into piles. When the family saw him, they all stopped work.

"About time too," said Dad, mopping his brow. "Where's that crate?"

Roy thought he'd change the subject. "Well done, Dad. Glad to see you decided to Dig for Victory after all."

Dad said nothing, but he breathed heavily.

"Where is it?" barked Gran. She was sitting on a wheelbarrow, directing operations. "We've got the hole ready."

"I've hidden it in Saint Cuthbert's," said Roy warily. "It's quite safe."

"You've hidden it in Saint Cuthbert's," Dad repeated, throwing down his spade. "Why?"

"I was chased by Boggy. I had to hide it somewhere. I'm sorry, but I didn't want to go to prison. It was the fruit or me."

There was a long silence. Obviously everyone would have preferred the fruit.

"I've been walking all night. I'm

exhausted," Roy gabbled. "It's quite safe –
Lenny can pick it up later."

Still no one said anything.

Roy tried to strike a cheerful note. "Look
at all the potatoes and carrots you've dug up.
We can have them for dinner."

Dad was the first to find his voice. "I
sometimes wonder how on earth you can be a
Pitt. Was he swopped by fairies while you
were standing in a queue, Ma?"

Ma shook her head sadly, and picked up
some of the vegetables. Roy followed her
example. Slowly, the rest of the family joined
them until only Gran remained aloof, watching
from her wheelbarrow throne, with an
expression of disgust.

Chapter 7

Roy Makes an Escape

At the centre of the table sat a large dish piled high with boiled carrots and parsnips.

On one side of it lay a bowl containing a solid mound of grey mashed potato.

On the other side, a lump of bread squatted on a cracked plate.

The Pitts sat in gloomy silence, gazing at their meal.

The door crashed open.

"Hello – it's only me." Mrs Moan barged into the room, dragging Hubert after her. There were sticky marks around his pasty mouth.

"Sorry to interrupt your dinner," she chirped.

The Pitts said nothing – they remained sunk in gloom.

Remembering his manners, Roy rose to his feet. "Would you like some mashed potato, Mrs Moa . . . er . . . Mrs Moon?"

"Ta ever so, but I couldn't manage it. Not after eating all that pineapple."

"Pineapple!"

"Yes. They took us all to shelter at Saint Cuthbert's Church last night. The ladies from the Women's Voluntary Service were ever so good. They gave us some soup –"

"Oxtail," said Hubert.

"Then we all sang songs, and Mr Gill, the fishmonger, told lots of jokes. Oh, he *is* a funny man. He laughs all the time."

"I'm not surprised, given the price of cod," sniffed Ma.

Mrs Moan rattled on, paying no attention to Ma. "Then the verger came in and said he'd found a crate of tinned fruit in the vestry, so we all said 'Pull the other one'. But it was true, because they gave us some lovely pineapple chunks –"

"With evaporated milk." Hubert licked his lips.

"Then they said it still wasn't safe to go home, so they made up beds in the pews and we stayed there all night. Then for breakfast we had some peaches. The Vicar said that things moved in a mysterious way, and we all laughed again. Then we had some more fruit. Hubert ate so much, he was sick. Weren't you, Hubert?"

Hubert nodded. "Twice."

"It was smashing. Oh well, glad to see you all so perky. Must be off. Bye for now."

There was a long silence, then Ma started to cry.

With an angry grunt, Dad rose from his chair and scowled at the plates of vegetables on the table.

"Pineapple," said Joanie, with a catch in her voice. "Peaches!"

"What *is* a peach?" asked Heather.

Lenny stabbed a carrot viciously and glared at Roy. "It's three years since I *saw* a pineapple."

Gran tightened the grip on her stick.

Roy shifted uneasily from foot to foot. He was surrounded by a circle of unfriendly eyes. "The Government says there's more goodness in root vegetables than in any other type of food."

Dad looked thoughtfully at Roy for a long time. Then, pushing aside his untouched plate of six carrots, three parsnips and a lump of mashed potato, he slowly began to unbuckle his belt.

Roy backed towards the door. He thought it might be a good idea if he moved in a mysterious way too.

Fast.

After all, there was no shame in running away. If he was in the army, it would be called making a tactical retreat. It was done all the time if the enemy forces were larger than yours.

And Dad was a lot larger than him.

Roy made a tactical retreat . . .

NOTES

Food Rationing

During the Second World War (1939 – 1945), German U-boats (submarines) sank many ships bringing food supplies to Britain. To make sure that food was fairly shared out, everyone in the country, even King George VI, had a ration book full of coupons. Shopkeepers tore out coupons, took the required money, and gave food in return. Butter, jam, meat, cheese, fresh eggs, sugar and sweets were all rationed at some time.

Funny Food

People got used to eating a lot of strange food during the war. Horse meat, whale meat, barracuda, were all on sale – as were unusual cuts of meat. Sheeps' heads, hearts and brains were not rationed – nor were pigs' trotters.

The Government encouraged people to gather free food from the countryside. Magazines provided recipes for dishes made from nuts, nettles, mushrooms, seaweed, dandelion leaves, rosehips and acorns.

The Dig For Victory Campaign

The Government urged people to grow vegetables anywhere they could. People sacrificed their lawns and flowerbeds to make vegetable gardens. Bomb sites, golf courses, parks and rubbish tips were all dug up to create allotments – small pieces of land rented to local people. By 1943 there were 3.5 million allotments in Britain.

Health

When war broke out many families were very poor and ate badly. Food rationing actually improved people's diet, because they were forced to cut down on fatty foods, like butter, lard and meat, and too many sweet things.

Instead they ate more fresh vegetables, because these were unrationed.

A "Vitamin Welfare" scheme began in December 1941, and children under two years old were issued with free blackcurrant juice and cod-liver oil. Later in the war, the blackcurrant juice was changed to orange juice.

The Black Market

Throughout the war, a thriving underground black market operated. Almost everyone knew someone who could get hold of some scarce or rationed item if the price was right. Many black marketeers became very rich, though if they were caught they could be fined and sent to prison.

The Pitt Family

Gran

Dad

Joanie

Lenny

Ma

Heather

Roy

Find out more about how the Pitts survived the Second World War.

Put That Light Out! 0 7496 3867 2 (Hbk)   0 7496 3961 X (Pbk)

Dad's fallen down a bomb crater! Lenny's walked into a lamp post! The Pitt family is having trouble in the blackout. Then the air-raid siren goes off . . .

Careless Talk 0 7496 3902 4 (Hbk)   0 7496 4009 X (Pbk)

A newcomer has arrived in Balaclava Terrace. He speaks with a foreign accent. He's got a small moustache. Is he a German spy?

Make Do and Mend 0 7496 3903 2 (Hbk)   0 7496 4010 3 (Pbk)

The Pitts are fed up with clothes rationing. They've nothing left to wear. Then Roy obtains a parachute, and the trouble begins . . .